Can I Get There From My Room?

By Elizabeth Lewis

Illustrated by
Bruce Lemerise

A GOLDEN BOOK • NEW YORK
Western Publishing Company, Inc., Racine, Wisconsin 53404

Michael was a terrific boy in many ways.
He was smart, strong, he had good friends,
and he made decisions very carefully.

But Michael had one fault. He was moody.
There were some days when Michael did not
want to do anything.

On this sunny Saturday morning in June there was more going on outside Michael's room than inside.

Outside, it was a busy summer day.

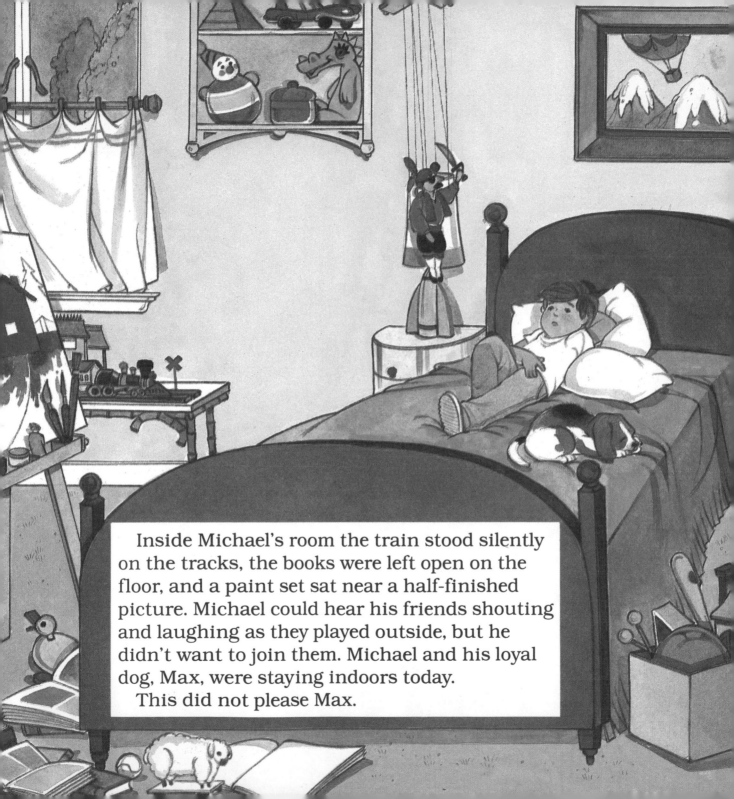

Inside Michael's room the train stood silently on the tracks, the books were left open on the floor, and a paint set sat near a half-finished picture. Michael could hear his friends shouting and laughing as they played outside, but he didn't want to join them. Michael and his loyal dog, Max, were staying indoors today.

This did not please Max.

"Aren't you going out today?" asked his mother through the door to his room.

"No," answered Michael.

"Why not?"

"Because I'm not leaving my room today, that's why."

"Well, wouldn't Max like to go outside?"

Yes, Max did want to go out. He had already tried to make Michael play, but finally gave up and sat down on his favorite rug. He had seen Michael like this before. Michael would play soon, but when?

"No, Max is staying with me," Michael said. "Right, Max?"

"Are you going to paint?" asked his mother.
"No, I like clay modeling now."

"Are you going to play with your train?"
"No, I'm bored with my train."

"Will you be reading your books?"
"I read them last week."

"Then you must be waiting for Sam to come over today."

"Sam is a dope!" said Michael.

"Michael, why would you want to just sit in your room on a beautiful sunny day?"

"Because!" shouted Michael. "I don't want to leave my room, and that's that."

"I thought you were planning a trip to the
moon today," said his mother.

"Can I get there from my room?" asked Michael.
"I'll go if I can get there from my room."

"Your room?" His mother was very surprised.
"I suppose if you put on your space helmet and
space suit you could get to the moon from
your room."

Michael looked at his space suit and helmet lying in a heap in the corner of his room. He remembered the day he and Max pretended they were the world's most famous astronauts.

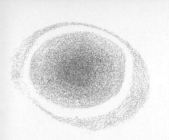

"No, not today," said Michael, shaking his head. "I'm tired of going to the moon."

"Yesterday you said that you and Max were going to the Wild West."

"Can I get there from my room?"

Michael's mother did not answer his question this time. He looked at the cowboy hat hanging on the rack in his room and thought about the day he pretended he was a cowboy. He and Max saw holdup men robbing people in a stagecoach. They ran to the rescue and were heroes.

"No, not today," said Michael. "I want to go someplace new, and I want to go there from my room."

"That's silly," said his mother.

"No, it's not," said Michael.

Max decided to take a nap until Michael changed his mind.

Michael looked at Max, who started making small whimpering noises in his sleep. His ears and tail were twitching. Max was dreaming about running in the country.

"Michael," said his mother, "you can't just sit in your room when there are so many places to explore and things to do!"

"Like where? Like what?" asked Michael.

"How about the circus? You enjoyed it last year."

"Can I get there from my room?"

"You should stop asking that silly question," said his mother. "Going to the circus is not like pretending to go to the moon or the Wild West. It's fun to be in the tent with all the other children, hearing music and cheering the circus acts."

Michael thought about everything he had seen at the circus.

"No, I don't think I'll be going out today,"
he said.

"Well, then, what are you going to do in your
room all day long?"

"Think."

"Why don't you think at Willow's Pond?"

"I can't get there from my room."

"Michael, it would be much better to walk there
with Max," said his mother crossly. "You could
fish while you lie under a willow tree."

Max thought this was a wonderful idea, but Michael was not so sure.

"What if there are no fish? Besides, I can't think and fish at the same time."

"Humph!" said his mother. "Then I have no ideas."

Michael and Max sat in silence. It would have to be a pretty special event to get Michael out today.

Suddenly, Max ran to the window barking. Sam was out there with a new boy that Michael had never seen before.

"Hey, Mickey, this is Arthur," Sam yelled up. "His family just moved here and his dad is building a treehouse in his yard. So come on out!"

"A treehouse!" said Michael. Now that appealed to him. "Neat-o! I'll be out in five seconds!"

Michael, Max, Sam, and Arthur ran all the way to Arthur's backyard. They spent the morning helping Arthur's dad finish building. They sawed and hammered and sawed.

"We could start a club and have secret meetings up here," said Michael, as they finally climbed inside.

"We could be private detectives," said Arthur, "and this could be our office!"

"We could bring our sleeping bags, and stay all night," said Sam.

The boys played together all day, and Michael had a great time.

"Just think, Max," said Michael on their way home. "We have a new friend, and Sam, you, and I will be going to play with him in his treehouse all the time now. I sure can't get *there* from my room…but who cares!"